Ever since I can remember . . .
I've dreamed of flying.

*Riiiiing!*

The last school bell of the year announced the start of summer —
days that stretched out lazily ahead.
I snapped my notebook shut on the pages
where I was doodling flying machines.

My parents did not approve.
"Get your head out of the clouds, Emery!"
they always told me. "Be practical!"

So I only told Mirabelle, my pet swallow,
about my ideas for fabulous inventions.

# Cloud
## CHASER

WRITTEN BY Anne-Fleur Drillon

ILLUSTRATED BY Eric Puybaret

TRANSLATED BY Lisa Rosinsky

We lived in the middle of a huge field
surrounded by olive trees,
at the edge of the ocean.
Seagulls flew high and lonely over the cliffs.

There was also the white house next door,
but no one lived there.
Until one summer evening,
a mysterious man moved in . . .

This man wore a wide-brimmed hat
and had a long white beard.
He unpacked a heap of strange objects
and piled them up in his garden.

Pressed against my window,
I watched him stroll among the towers of junk,
mumbling to himself, for hours.

My parents said, "Look, a new friend!
Why don't we all go and say hello?"

But I was too shy.

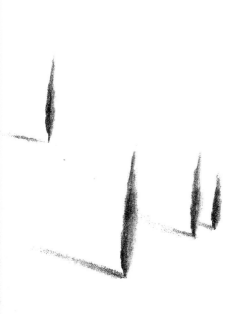

One morning, not seeing the shadow of his black hat,
I crept over to his garden.
I couldn't help exploring the jumble of amazing objects —
who knew what might be in there?
Like Mirabelle digging for a juicy worm,
I rummaged through the clutter.

And then,
underneath some old newspapers,
I found treasure . . . a go-kart!
Nearby was a trunk
filled with rolls of wallpaper.
In a flash, it hit me — these were exactly
the items I needed to build the machine of the century!

I took the supplies to the field
and worked all day, losing track of time,
until finally,
the **WING WIZARD**
was born.

I puffed out my chest,
as proud as Mirabelle when she sang one of her songs.
I climbed inside my invention
and began to push the pedals.

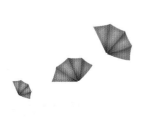

Suddenly, I saw him —
the strange old man.
He ran towards me,
an enormous object in his arms.

What was he carrying?
And why?
Was he going to throw something at me?
Chase me away?

"Hello, there!" he cried.

"You won't get very far like that!

Painted paper wings —

those won't be enough to lift anyone into the sky.

You need stronger wings,

and you need to go faster.

Let's try this."

He showed me what he carried.

It was a propeller!

"With the propeller,

you can go faster," he explained,

"and maybe get enough air

under those wings."

His pockets were heavy with tools, too.

He spent the rest of the afternoon

showing me how to use them.

By evening, the **WING WIZARD**

had been transformed.

Grabbing the steering wheel,

I tried to turn the propeller, but it was rusty and stuck.

I twisted the wheel until the car tipped right over,

and I fell out into the grass.

We both burst out laughing.

"By the way, my name is Leon,"
    he said, as he helped me up.

"I'm Emery," I said.
    "And this is my swallow, Mirabelle.
    We've never met another
        inventor before!"

From that day on,
    we worked on our inventions
        together every day.
My parents still shook their heads at me,
        but they invited Leon over for tea.
They were glad I'd found a friend.
Leon and I rummaged for hours in his garden.
    Each object we found gave us new ideas.

"We still need stronger wings . . .
    Now, what can we do with these
        old bicycle wheels?" he asked.

I held up a piece of fabric.

    "Yes!" he shouted.
        "That's it! You will soar over the fields!"

We took the spokes off the wheels and
    sewed them into the fabric, to make a wing
        that held its shape but was still flexible.

And that's how
the SKY CLIMBER
came into being.

The propeller got me going fast enough to
push a lot of air under the wings.
This time, I got off the ground,
but crash-landed in an olive tree . . .

Over the next two months,
I banged into sixteen tree trunks,
thumped into eight rosebushes
and came nose-to-nose
with three startled seagulls.

Leon was there to rescue me every time.

One afternoon, when we were messing around
with a piece of laundry line,
I heard Mirabelle singing from a branch above us.

"Leon!" I cried. "That's it!"

I called her name and she flew down to my arm.

Mirabelle held very still while we carefully measured her wings.
Then Leon scampered away like a rabbit, reappearing with
the motor from a lawnmower and two gigantic fans.
He showed me how to cut them, and we worked together,
whistling Mirabelle's tune.

The CLOUD CHASER
was the most beautiful machine
ever invented!
As the motor roared to life,
the machine began to pick up speed.
I felt the ground disappear beneath me.
The wind whipped my face,
and the seagulls fled.
Leon was a tiny speck on the ground,
far below me. He waved his arms.
Squinting, I could see his mouth
stretched into a huge smile.
I was on top of the world!

Until . . . CRASH!

When I opened my eyes,
I was perched on the roof.
But I was fine,
and so was the CLOUD CHASER.

"It only needs some tinkering
and fine-tuning!" Leon hollered.
"Believe me, this machine will work!"

We spent the rest of the summer
    working on our flying machine,
        measuring, adjusting,
    adding a few hooks here,
        a few clips there . . .

I wished I could freeze those moments in time,
    so they would never come to an end.
        Those afternoons,
            I was no longer just a kid,
        dreaming and doodling.

We were adventurers.

    We were inventors of happiness.

But on soft feet,
     the summer crept to an end,
swapping laughter and warm breezes
     for my coat and schoolbag.

I saw Leon less often.

          And then one day,
               he disappeared.

**I found a note pinned to his door:**

*Dear Emery,*

*At last, we have tamed the* **CLOUD CHASER***!*
*I've been called away on important business across the sea . . .*
*So on this lovely autumn morning, I shall strap on my helmet,*
*snap my goggles into place,*
*and take our invention on its first trip over the ocean.*

*You must keep working on your own creations,*
*and when I return, we will fly together.*
*Wish me luck on the journey . . .*

*— Leon*

Wherever Leon had gone,

      I knew he would need company.

So I set Mirabelle free to find him.

In the meantime,

      I doodle ideas in my notebook

and work in the field between our houses

      with Leon's tools.

Someday,

      on the wings

         of a warm summer breeze,

my friend will come back

      in our first-ever flying machine.

And I will show him all my newest inventions.

# For Damien and Armelle — E. P.

Barefoot Books
2067 Massachusetts Ave
Cambridge, MA 02140

Barefoot Books
29/30 Fitzroy Square
London, W1T 6LQ

Graphic design by Sarah Soldano, Barefoot Books
English-language edition edited by Lisa Rosinsky, Barefoot Books
Aeronautics consultation by Nivair H. Gabriel, Barefoot Books
First published in Great Britain by Barefoot Books, Ltd and in the
United States of America by Barefoot Books, Inc in 2018
All rights reserved

Reproduction by Bright Arts, Hong Kong
Printed in China on 100% acid-free paper
This book was typeset in Bembo,
Blockhead and FogtwoNo5
The illustrations were prepared in acrylics

Hardback ISBN: 978-1-78285-411-1
Paperback ISBN: 978-1-78285-412-8

British Cataloguing-in-Publication Data:
a catalogue record for this book is
available from the British Library

Library of Congress Cataloging-in-Publication Data
is available upon request

1 3 5 7 9 8 6 4 2